Diary of a Wallflower

A Poetry Chapbook

By

Jalisa Ogundelu

Death of a Wallflower Copyright © 2023 Jalisa Ogundelu

All rights reserved.

No portion of this book may be reproduced in any form without written permission from the publisher or author, except as permitted by copyright law

ISBN: 9798857226568

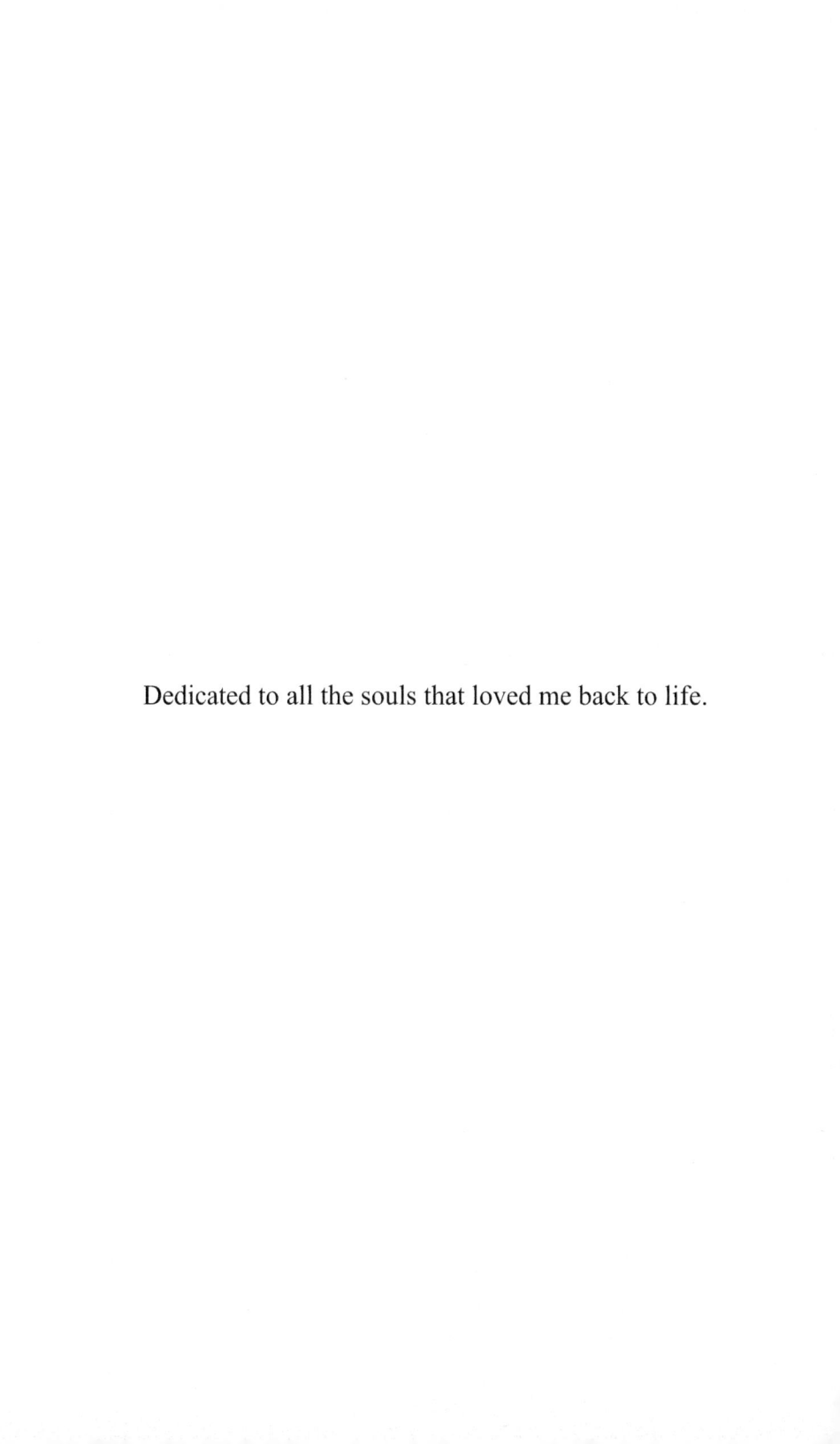

Dedicated to all the souls that loved me back to life.

TABLE OF CONTENTS

1	Queen of Nowhere	Pg 1
2	Smells like Spring	Pg 3
3	Jasmine's World	Pg 5
4	The Life and Crimes of a Slug	Pg 7
5	Wingin' it	Pg 9
6	Stalker	Pg 10
7	Lemon and Honey	Pg 12
8	Apples and Oranges	Pg 14
9	The Picnic	Pg 16
10	A flower without petals	Pg 18
11	Daisy Chains	Pg 21
12	Diggin'	Pg 23
13	A sunny disposition	Pg 24
14	Asylum	Pg 25
15	Words of Prey	Pg 27
16	Ode to the Moon	Pg 28
17	Wallflower's Elegy	Pg 30

18	What remains	Pg 33
19	Ophelia and the Love Me Not's	Pg 35
20	The Cleanse	Pg 36
21	Cherry blossom	Pg 37
22	Kissed a frog today	Pg 38
23	Dandelions	Pg 40
24	Watering Can's Observations	Pg 41
25	Choices	Pg 43
26	My Significant Other	Pg 44
27	Sunlight for breakfast	Pg 47
28	Butterflies don't speak	Pg 48
29	Like Flower, Like Sun	Pg 51
30	Queen of Somewhere	Pg 53
	Thank you	
	About the Author	

"Nature does not hurry, yet everything is accomplished."

- Lao Tzu

Queen of Nowhere

Come, let me fill your pretty skull with secrets.

Please, make yourself at home.

What's mine is yours, for you're my guest,

But leave your questions at the door.

If you want to know where you are

Perhaps I'll give you a clue.

It's a place that no one else could find.

But in your mind's eye, lives to be true.

I'm the Queen of Nowhere.

Lost in translation, as the saying goes.

I'm a widow of hope, survived by tragedy.

My black heart has cast a miserable spell,

And now, only cobwebs and weeds grow.

My subjects are frozen in time.

For my reign has sucked the colour from this place,

And now I only see sadness, death and disgrace.

You're not the only passerby to wander through these

Strange lands. It was fate.

Curiosity helped you find this lost kingdom of mine.

Take my hand. Hold your breath,

And let me fill your pretty skull with secrets.

Smells like Spring

Have you stopped to smell the roses recently?

They smell like spring. In fact, when I close my eyes

I see the sun with a cheeky smile,

Peeking through the trees

As the cold air begins, to whisper its goodbye.

When I touch their petals, I feel soft pillows

As the soft orange glow pours in through the window,

Kissing my cheek, asking me to wake up

So I can greet the new day.

For spring was always meant to be.

It's a light eau de parfum that Mother Nature likes to wear

First thing in the morning.

A bright and fruity scent,

Like cutting into fresh strawberries.

Something sweet in the air,

A quiet pleasure slowly dawning.

As I close my eyes, I hear the birds, singing with their

brilliant melodies.

I sink my feet into the earth, curling my toes around the

Dewy sticky grass,

Drinking in the pale blue sky.

There's a spring in my step,

As I walk towards the white roses.

For my dreams are still ripe,

And my desires hang within my grasp,

For it will always smell like spring,

When I'm wide awake in the dark.

Jasmine's World

My first memory

Is of Jasmine.

When I look at the lake

Through her eyes

I see Jasmine.

When I open my mouth to speak

I hear Jasmine.

And I'd use my last breath

To wish to be Jasmine.

Looking back

That's why I wanted to be near Jasmine;

I was hoping some of Jasmine would rub off on me.

In all honesty

Jasmine was the song I was meant to sing.

It would be so nice to escape

Into Jasmine's world.

Spend a day in the life.

I'd rather deal with Jasmine's problems

For Jasmine bloomed so early.

The sun shows Jasmine love,

And I'd rather be Jasmine,

Than live another day as a wallflower.

The Life and Crimes of a Slug

There once was a slug named Paul.

He hadn't much luck at all.

He'd try to move on,

But he'd be back at square one,

And the distance he made was small.

Paul knew not from where his bad luck came.

He did not have anyone to blame.

But himself for being slow,

Whilst the flowers around him grow,

And a stalled slug he remained.

Paul was not wanted here you see.

He'd been at the lettuce again for free.

He knew The Gardener would be back,

And The Gardener would be mad,

When he saw Paul's lettuce killing spree.

And Paul wasn't the best at hiding his tracks.

For perspiration would sweat off his back.

It would leave a glistening trail,

The Gardener would find him without fail,

And salt would begin its fatal attack.

Alas, this was the price to be paid.

A sinner hunger had made.

And Paul's great escape,

Would not be so great,

Because he couldn't get his legs to obey.

Then suddenly there were footsteps he heard,

The end was near, The Gardener and his salt had returned!

If only he wasn't so slow,

Now to hell he would go,

Oh well, perhaps in the next life he'd be a cheetah.

Wingin' it

Don't know what you were expecting from coming here but don't look at me - I'm no good with directions. I just go where the wind blows sometimes that's north, sometimes that's south, so who on earth knows where it will take me next? I once had a flock I used to fly with. I was supposed to travel the world with them but my wings didn't grow in time. When I finally left the nest they had all gone. That was years ago. Time flies I suppose. So I spend my days all over the place for they say seek and you shall find, not quite sure what I'm looking for though, perhaps one day I'll find my tribe but in the meantime, I quite enjoy catching worms and, in the last few months, I've found a spot by a brick wall where seeds are left for me.

Stalker

You wanted to spill my blood.

For blood is not thicker than water

And this time, the tip of your knife found my organs.

And I suppose you're singing your praises.

Oh, how I'd love to strain your vocal cords.

And then you wouldn't spit so much poison.

Twisting my words until they start to slither and hiss.

Don't you get tired of this?

You've crept up on me before,

Somehow I never see you coming.

I'm usually too blinded by my daydreams instead,

Plotting your downfall in my head.

You're the reason I'm a stigma.

You're the reason why they all have cuts on their fingers.

I want them to witness a rose in full bloom.

But your jealousy possesses me

And I'm doomed

To live life, with a thorn in my side.

So, I'll suffer this blow,

Because we both know,

That I've let you get away with murder again.

We've got seven wounded, and twenty-three dead

Are you proud of yourself?

You've painted my whole world red.

I hope you don't expect me to clean up this bloody mess.

I hope you know this story will soon end...

Lemon and Honey

I don't know what it is with these two.

Can't live with or without each other,

There's always something new.

Lemon comes to me and starts moaning

About how things have gone sour.

Again. They'd only kissed and made up about an hour

Ago.

Honey thinks Lemon constantly criticises her.

Honey wants Lemon in small doses

Or it all becomes a pain.

But Lemon thinks it's healthy to be harsh with the tongue.

Life is harsh, as it should be.

So you can wake up

And get to where the hell you need to be.

Honey's feelings are hurt and she's threatening to leave.

Because every time she tries to make something sweet,

Lemon comes along and just spoils the treat.

DEATH OF A WALLFLOWER

Always has to be bright and bold and in control.

Honey knows that you can't always hide in a jar

But that doesn't mean you've failed in life,

Just because you didn't get very far.

Lemon disagrees.

Lemon's been out in the wild.

Lemon lived in nature. Growing on trees.

Honey's gotten too used to the bees always helping her.

Everyone's always doting, saying how sweet she is.

If someone knocked Honey over she'd stick to the floor.

Doesn't know how to get up.

Lemon claims he'd beat them to a pulp.

And he's always got extra seeds to spread

In the unlikely event of his death.

I don't know what it is with these two,

They just don't go together.

But I suppose that's why they do.

Apples and Oranges

You had barely wiped the juice off your lips,

Before you left my bed that cold summer morning

And ran straight into her arms.

Does that mean I tasted like nothing?

You told me,

That I was the sweetest thing you'd ever tasted,

That I was the apple of your eye.

That my skin was the smoothest.

And when you held me, your fingers burned with pleasure.

In your own words, it was like, "Holding the sun."

So, was I the moon then?

Forever in her shadow,

Trying to get the last scraps of shine.

After all this time I spent, waiting for you to pick me.

I could not quite satisfy you,

And you needed something sweeter.

Do you enjoy chewing up innocent hearts?

DEATH OF A WALLFLOWER

What's her secret?

Does she have more layers to peel?

More secrets to reveal?

Instead of tasting the truth in one bite?

I can feel the winds of autumn coming.

I'm hanging from this tree by a thread.

I'll end this misery myself, and cut the rope.

I hope you enjoy your chosen one, my friend.

The Picnic

Which is it?

Would you like to sit in the sun or the shade?

Do you want to sin in daylight or the dark today?

Which is it?

The water or the wine?

Do you want to be sober or drunk whilst we dine?

Which is it?

For this last supper,

Do you want poisoned berries or strawberries?

Do you choose silence or do you have more to say to me?

Which is it?

Would you like some cutlery or a napkin perhaps?

Are you going to use a knife and fork,

Or tear me to shreds with your bare hands?

So which is it?

Can I get you anything else,

Before you feast on my esteem?

No?

Ok, let's just say a quick prayer before we eat.

A flower without petals

A red dress hugs her flesh like a glove.

Hips sway this way that way, curls cascade, red waterfalls.

But be careful.

For she's thirsty for blood.

She hides thorns in her purse.

And she stems from infected soil.

Her smile is like the break of dawn,

Yellow shining on a sinner's soul,

Planting yellow seeds of hope on your lips,

Like the sun itself kissed you!

But be careful.

She droops when she's forced to wear night shade's purple

Cloak. And the tears will come soon.

For her true colours will show.

She likes to wear lavender perfume,

She sprays it on her collarbone.

Men in yellow and black line up,

Just to get a whiff of her scent.

But be careful.

They can't have her.

And neither can you.

No matter how much you beg.

She can't hear you - her ears are full of wax,

And her words will sting.

She loves to float on the water,

Watching the frogs, in a lily-white dress,

So innocent is she,

As she witnesses the scene with glee,

But be careful.

She'll start to sing to you.

Wanting to marry you at this very moment.

But those who've followed her down the aisle,

Drowned at their own wedding.

Her body is a graveyard and her mind is full of weeds.

Her petals were snatched many moons ago.

And it haunts her in her sleep.

She soothes her wounds by wandering the earth.

Changing colours whenever need be.

Brushing off the flies from her lips.

To tell you, "You're the one for me."

A flower without petals,

What a cruel joke. Lost was her identity.

But she doesn't want your sympathy;

She's the one stealing petals now,

And the world will soon fall at her feet.

Daisy Chains

Hands reaching out to me,

Ready to grasp my neck,

And drag me out from the grass,

I was hiding in plain sight I guess.

You don't speak my language, you're not from here.

Something in the dead look in your eyes

Tells me, that you don't care,

That you don't speak with love,

That your breath stinks of nightmares.

I hear chains clash in the distance,

And I try to run away.

I'd heard that you'd been plucking us,

And I don't want to be your slave.

But now it's too late. The grass is blackened and burning,

My home is ruined now, and my freedom is slipping away.

I'm an orphan, but I don't want to join the others,

I don't want to share their fate.

Something has caught my hand,

And the ground crashes into my face,

I feel something pierce my flesh and cry out,

A hole in my body, in my heart's place.

Marked. I feel a stranger on top of me,

There's no privacy, no pride.

We're entwined. Forced to be intimate.

But we're not from the same tribe.

I look around and see a dozen other faces,

That look just like mine.

Screams won't save me now,

My limbs have been ripped from their bones,

And all you care to do is sing, sing, sing!

I'll never see home again.

I'll live and die in these daisy chains.

Diggin'

Diggin' ain't easy. You know that. But it's not

Even about the diggin'. You're just stuck in the mud. The

Plan was to plant seeds. Grow flowers. But your

Reality is hell. Nothing grows in a graveyard. You can't

Even stop diggin' when it hurts. Got to keep diggin'

So you can finally sleep. Weeds, worms, wasps -

Something's rotting in this soil. You're killing time,

It's all you know. You have to dig, dig, dig! It's the

Only way. Gotta eat, so you gotta dig, but you want

Nothing more than to feel alive.

A sunny disposition

There comes a time

When the sun doesn't want to smile anymore.

It gets tired of being bright all day.

Exhausted from the energy it takes,

To live up to this image that was created.

It rolls over and shows the world its back.

For it's been pretending for too long.

The sun would cry itself to sleep if it could,

But it made a promise to the weather that it wouldn't rain.

So just remember,

When you open up your curtains

And see the sun rise once more.

It doesn't always want to be there,

But it fought every bone in its body to get out of bed,

And shine for you.

That's for sure.

Asylum

Twisted and tangled are these never-ending days,

Underneath the earth,

Where the human eye could not see.

Surrounded by ungodly creatures,

Drooling like zombies, spines contorted, legs bruised.

Doomed to stay in this wet dark womb.

Hoping not to get strangled by the roots.

Before we all retreat to our revolving doors for the

Never-ending night.

Drops drip from the ends of tubes.

We've finally been watered by the nurse.

Funny that, I barely see her.

Veins of the earth, spiralling like a staircase.

Down the corridors their promises echo,

But they're muffled by the resident's

Psychotic screams of sorrow.

For how deep into the past must we dig,

To finally find our tomorrow?

It's easy to say just wait a little longer,

But when you're stuck in the mud,

The more you wait, the more you suffer.

And I've heard whispers of what the sun looks like.

And I want to see for myself, like the others.

But, when The Gardener's spade hits us like an earthquake,

And the seeds are sown,

It's a waiting game, to see if our souls will blossom,

Or if we're doomed to eternally suffocate,

In the soils of the asylum.

Words of Prey

Twittering on the phone,

A birdsong of troubles and woes.

Hatching curses in your speech,

They soar out of your beak.

Loathsome phrases, winged and eagle-eyed,

Around my head they glide;

The target they have spied.

A flock of your disdain,

Talons descending on my brain,

Black feathers rustle as they feast:

Your vicious words of prey.

Ode to the Moon

We are the nocturnal animals:

Lost souls,

Out of sync with the rhythm of the waking world,

Wondering how it came to this,

Trying to remember a time without emptiness.

Since the sun shut the door on our empty plight,

We're doomed to dance for our master: Mr. Night.

I sing songs of sorrow to him,

But I don't think he cares to hear my wails.

I'd love to escape, from this hellish place,

But my wings have been clipped

And my feet are in chains.

I know you feel it too,

Together we live in exile, in the depths of solitude.

Where your screams are stolen by the silence.

Haunted, taunted, tormented in conspicuous violence.

For you're not the only one that's cursed to live like this.

DEATH OF A WALLFLOWER

It's like we don't exist -

Never loved, never wanted, never remembered.

No choice but to dress in black.

Our old friend Darkness has made sure of that.

You thought no one would notice,

But I've had my big brown eyes on you.

I see you shivering in your sleep

You have the same nightmares that I do.

You gave birth to the sun,

But the sun has not been so kind to you,

And now you've got a case of the post-partum blues.

O' sweet moon,

Don't dry your tears.

Come down here, let's weep together.

Like me, you once had stars in your eyes,

But let's mourn the day we lost the light in our lives,

And at least we'll have each other.

Wallflower's Elegy

My dearest wallflower,

Loving you was painful.

I tasted blood every time I tried to speak,

And more scars appeared when we embraced.

Loving you was painful.

I tried to pick up the broken mirror shards,

But then I got a glimpse

And I'd punch you instead, and it left me black and blue.

I wanted to kiss you

Believe me,

I wanted to give you tenderness and honey

To soothe those open wounds,

That ooze tears with every move.

Yet loving you

Left me black and blue

Because loving you was painful.

Believe me,

DEATH OF A WALLFLOWER

I've tried to let my fingertips rest

On your stem. I've asked you to undress

But what do I get?

More blood, more mess.

You are not what you seem.

Behind your invisible cloak

Are things no one could ever dream.

I guess that's what you mean,

When you say, "No one ever sees me."

Open up and I'd baptise you with my blood,

But instead, you keep your legs shut

Mouth closed, eyes open.

Thorny legs cut me down every time I try to touch

You.

So,

I had to do it.

I'm not afraid to confess my crimes.

You've returned to the dirt. Where you belong.

Because loving you was painful.

Now I am free

I'll see what else life has in store for me.

Yours Sincerely,

The Gardener.

What remains

Once the flower pot is shattered,

Into a thousand tiny pieces,

It may seem as if all that mattered,

Can never be put back together.

All the seeds of hope and the memories you planted,

And the dreams and spuds you watered,

That called the flower pot home,

Now exposed,

All over the floor,

A puddle of soil and ash.

Putting it all back together again,

Floods you with overwhelm,

It's too much to bear,

When the long days have worn you down,

And the flower pot carried the little hope you had left.

But when the flower pot falls apart,

That does not spell the end.

The rain will try to drown you,

And the thorns will try to cut you,

But when you realise they can't kill you,

You know that you can go on.

Piece by piece, day by day,

The flower pot pieces will be put back together again.

It will never look the same,

You can see the wrinkles, the cracks, the bruises, the

Pain.

But the flower pot will be happy to carry

Your seeds of hope once more,

For there is so much beauty

In what remains.

Ophelia and the Love Me Nots

What the water gave me,

Was a new way of life.

When it turned my lungs blue.

Washed away my stress and strife.

Weeds wrapped around my toes

Wishing for me to never leave the water's cold embrace.

Wanting me to rest on a bed of bones, a treasure chest.

Wrinkled and pale I'd become, as I sank to the seabed.

Written in my eyes was peace. As I found

Where the wallflower had been laid to rest.

The Cleanse

Undressed, I dip my toe into the furnace.

Ready to see if it's hot enough yet.

Hot showers of tears start to resurface.

I'm ready to release those memories I've repressed.

Shaking softly, I let the water seep through my skin.

Let's take notes now that I'm finally listening.

Wow! I'd forgotten those scars were still there.

Divorce, death, depression. Interesting. Interesting.

Fire is the only thing that cleanses me of these flashbacks.

Soap will never work.

I don't know what else to say

As I slip beneath,

Whispering in tongues,

Drowning on purpose,

Hoping for rebirth.

And then I'll get dressed for the day.

Cherry blossom

Cherry blossoms bloom

When the koi fish tells it to.

Earlier, would be too soon.

Kissed a frog today

Dear Diary,

The date is, well, the first day of summer.

I say that because with each day my flowers grow stronger

And the wallflower hasn't been seen since last September.

Anyway,

I kissed a frog today.

You see,

I was minding my own business pulling out the weeds,

Breaking a sweat since I'd let them overgrow,

And I was feeling dizzy. So I sat down, but then

I saw these two big black holes staring up at me.

And I'd always wanted to know

What frogs taste like!

So I got on my knees and gave it a go.

The novelty soon wore off though,

As soon as I felt the wet cold slime slip onto my tongue.

And get stuck in my throat,

I almost choked!

I've finished all the Listerine so

Maybe I'll have to drink some bleach.

But even once my mouth is clean

I'll never be able to wash off the taste.

But yeah, I kissed a frog today.

Oh well, that's why this is a secret diary.

So you better not go and tell anybody!

Dandelions

And as I opened my eyes,

I wondered if it had all been a bad dream.

Because once the fresh air came,

And I breathed hope into my lungs,

It was as if those thoughts began to turn to dust.

I cupped them in my hands,

Blew them one last kiss,

Made one last wish,

And gave them to the wind.

Watering Can's Observations

For a long time,

The Gardener would brew his tea at half nine.

He'd leave it on the window sill for hours,

But it struggled to survive in the cold, on its own.

Then, he would pick me up and fill me with icy water,

From the tap that sounded like it was dying of laughter.

To my disdain, I'd be planted next to his boots,

Shedding flakes of mud, dead skin, and soot.

Dry leaves knocked on the front door, calling us outside.

But, like his tea, I soon realised he'd forgotten about me.

Eek! The stairs would cry

As he dragged himself up to bed and back to sleep.

For his waking moments were haunted by bad dreams.

And when night came, he'd scream her name.

And then come downstairs in the morning,

To do it all again.

Except for today.

Once his cup of tea started crying out for company,

And he'd put some lukewarm water in me,

I saw him put on his boots for the first time, in a long time,

And step outside.

He looked for the patch of earth where she used to grow,

Reached into his pocket, and placed down a note

That read, "You were like air to me,

And I'm sorry to see you go,

But I've found other things that help me breathe."

So, perhaps he'll show his tea some love tomorrow.

Choices

Choices change their tune. To tempt flowers with

Options that no mortal could refuse. But

No one knows that when the peace is disturbed,

Flowers arm themselves with metal.

If the treachery continues they go to war to

Defend their homeland. It's no Garden of

Eden but the gates are closed to the

Naysayers that seek to secure the flower's downfall. The

Choices made today will be the final battle, and the

Enemy will soon discover the taste of metallic petals.

My Significant Other

I don't think you realise

You've stolen my heart

I need you here, just to keep living.

Because without you, I'm paralysed

And it feels like an organ is missing.

I don't think you realise

That your soul is the food I live off of and

When you're not here,

My spirit grows cold,

Without the warmth of its best friend.

I don't think you realise

That only your arms feel like home and

Your voice is the only language I speak.

Everything else is silent.

When we kiss, my heart stops for you.

And for a few sweet moments, my life is in your hands.

DEATH OF A WALLFLOWER

I don't think you realise,

I wouldn't be mad,

If you chose not to revive me.

You saved me from myself,

You helped me find my roots,

I can die in peace, knowing that you've healed my wounds.

But I don't want to go,

Not just yet.

Because I'll never find a love like this again.

I'm not sure if we came from the same seed,

Planted in the same soil,

But you're the only one who understands my story,

Without me needing to explain it all.

My demons know your face,

But still, you choose to love me,

And it's a love that sets me on fire:

It could never be replaced.

I don't think you realise,

That I'm still trying to find the courage to tell you all this,

Maybe one day,

You'll look in the mirror,

And realise that I'm truly blessed.

Sunlight for breakfast

When my belly is full

When the day's rollover

When I'm wishing for the sun

When the butterflies kick stronger and stronger

When my skin begins to break with sweat

When the expected brings the unexpected

When I'm sticky and screaming in ecstasy

So hard that I almost bite my tongue

And I hear your cry

That's when I know summer has been born.

Butterflies don't speak

If you've spoken to a butterfly and there was no response.

This means it simply wants

You to read between the lines for once.

For its wings are like a book of wisdom,

With answers on every page.

They're a testament to the strength it took.

To get through to the other side of yesterday.

If you look closely,

You'll notice that their story is still being written.

You can stay around long enough

To see if you'll be the friend, foe or villain.

They fly the flag for the country of lost souls

And they paint themselves in beautiful vivid colours,

A patchwork of painful memories drawn together,

To be a symbol, a badge of honour, for

The ones who managed to escape from the gutter.

And butterflies don't speak

Because they're asked so often about their past.

And it's become tiring speaking a caterpillar's language.

They would much rather spend time alone

Than be triggered

By the sordid memories of life being ugly, unwanted and Disfigured.

They're a sensitive species with lots of idiosyncrasies

And their antennae mean they pick up strange frequencies

Quite easily.

And to hear the rumours spread so carelessly

Hurts.

Of course, they wouldn't say anything.

Because butterflies don't speak.

But you'll hear about it later,

When butterflies decide to put pen to paper.

So,

Butterflies don't speak,

Because quite frankly,

There is no need.

And sometimes it's a story you'll need to see to believe.

It's one of loss, revelation and change.

And the butterflies would love to share it with you one day.

They'll try again next time.

If you stick out your hand.

They'll land on your finger.

No,

They still won't speak to you.

But they'll gently flap their wings,

And hopefully, you'll have a clue.

Of what the butterfly wants you to do.

Like Flower, Like Sun

Like flower, like sun.

We are one.

I've told you all along.

Not to run.

Look for me

And you will find.

Who you were meant to be.

I was always shining down on you.

You just couldn't see that

You needed me.

To rise.

Run towards my light,

Let me hold you tight.

And wipe away the rain.

On your cheeks.

It's your time to shine.

I'm glad you found your roots.

Sow your seeds,

And tomorrow you'll meet

The woman you were destined to be.

Queen of Somewhere

Surrounded by her ladybirds in waiting,

She makes her way up the winding stairs.

Fate has twisted into something else.

With each step she takes,

The chorus of the bluebells grows louder.

Her heart beats along with the trumpet's song and

A thousand beady eyes follow her

As she walks down the aisle.

Holding on to her bouquet for dear life,

She keeps her eyes on the prize and,

For the first time in her life,

Walks in a straight line.

She kneels before the priest, her head bent low in prayer,

As the wreath is finally placed on her head,

And she is crowned. All hail,

The Queen of Somewhere.

JALISA OGUNDELU

Hey there!

Thank you so much for reading my debut poetry chapbook. I hope you enjoyed reading it. I loved writing it!

Keep your eyes peeled for more work from me, this was just a taste of things to come.

Sending you lots of love,

Jalisa

JALISA OGUNDELU

ABOUT THE AUTHOR

Jalisa Ogundelu is a Black British poet based in London. Her first love is the written word, and she's been scribbling stories in journals and notebooks since she was in nappies. After picking up poetry in lockdown, Jalisa decided it was time to make a splash on the scene with her debut poetry chapbook: Death of a Wallflower.

Currently, in her early twenties, Jalisa is investing in personal development and learning about the world around her. When she's not writing, Jalisa enjoys: visiting new places, belly dancing, spending time in nature and fuelling her sugar addiction with chocolate.

To watch her poetry blossom, follow @jalisa_writes

Printed in Great Britain
by Amazon